Grandpa's Gizmos

John Menken

Illustrated by Tim Davis

Grandpa's Gizmos

Edited by Keith A. Skaggs

© 1992 Bob Jones University Press
Greenville, South Carolina 29614

Printed in the United States of America

ISBN 0-89084-663-4

20   19   18   17   16   15   14   13   12   11   10   9   8   7   6

To my family:
Beverly,
Joy, Dawn, and David

J. M.

The wind bloweth where it listeth, and thou
hearest the sound thereof, but canst not tell
whence it cometh, and whither it goeth.

John 3:8

It was my turn to visit Grandma and Grandpa Winslow.
When I got there, Grandpa Winslow was in his back yard
flying a bright yellow kite.

The wind blew his white hair in all directions,
but he didn't seem to mind. He stood there humming
as he watched his kite.

That kite frisked and skipped and danced across the sky.
It was just about the highest kite I had ever seen.

He gave me a kite too, but I couldn't get it to fly.
Grandpa saw that, I guess, and he let me hold the string of his kite
while he made mine go.

Then he showed me how to pull a little on the string
when my kite started to drop. He showed me how to let the string out
sl-o-o-w-ly so my kite would fly higher without flopping around
and falling out of the sky.

"How can you do that so well?" I asked him.

"Oh, I like to work with the wind."
He waved a hand at his back yard.

Now that my kite was flying pretty well,
I took a quick look around.
Grandpa must have taken a lot of time
to work with the wind.

He had a flagpole with three flags flying from it.
He had a gazebo with a windsock on its roof
and seven pinwheels on its rail.

He had a row of spinning bleach bottles on sticks
and a tree full of ribbons all blowing the same way.

"What are all those things?" I asked.

"Gizmos," he answered.

"What are they for?"

"I like things that work with the wind," he said.
"They let me see what the wind is doing.
And they keep me company."
He was still watching the kites dancing
high above us.

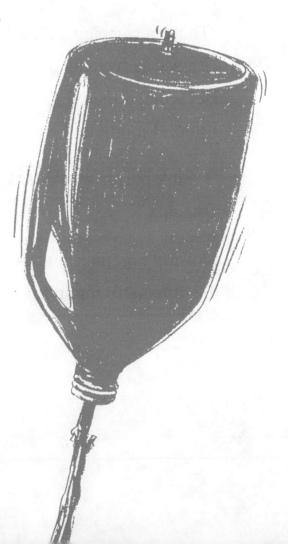

I glanced up at my kite and then
back at the tree full of ribbons.
"Is that a new kind of Christmas tree, Grandpa?" I asked.

"That's a weeping willow," he said.
"It used to have its own green streamers.
But when it died, I gave it those blue and white ones.
I think I might add purple too. What do you think?"

"I think purple would look good,
Grandpa."

Blowing together in the wind like that,
the streamers reminded me of waves on a lake.

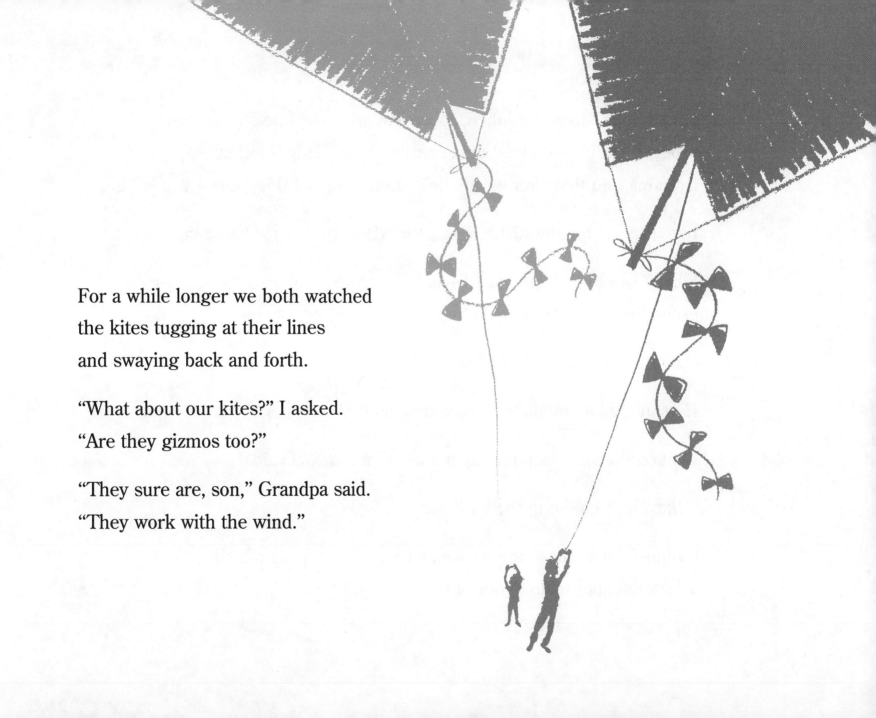

For a while longer we both watched
the kites tugging at their lines
and swaying back and forth.

"What about our kites?" I asked.
"Are they gizmos too?"

"They sure are, son," Grandpa said.
"They work with the wind."

Grandma called us for lunch; so we wound in the kite strings and brought the kites down. I didn't really want to stop then, but Grandpa said that after we ate he'd show me something else I would like.

I kept trying to guess what it was the whole time we were eating.

Finally Grandpa laughed and said, "Hurry up and finish those green beans and then you'll find out."

"Is it another gizmo, Grandpa?"

He squinted at my plate. "Are you all done?"

I poked the last bean into my mouth. "I'm done," I said.

"Okay, let's go out in the back yard."

I followed him out to the gazebo, where he pulled an old sheet off something I hadn't noticed before.

"Hey!" I said. "Is this a gizmo too, Grandpa?"

"Yep. See how the wind turns these paddlelike things here at the top? That moves the widget down here. Do you like it?"

"I sure do!"

"I thought you might. When I heard you were coming to visit, I made it just for you. Maybe we could keep it here next to the gazebo; what do you think?"

"Yes sir, Grandpa!"

We sat down next to my gizmo and talked.

I asked Grandpa about the wind and how it ran all those gizmos.

He told me that the wind could lift up a kite and spin a pinwheel at the same time. It could make waves in the streamer tree while it was working my gizmo's paddles.

"And that windsock is a useful gizmo," he added.

"It shows which way the wind is blowing."

Suddenly Grandpa said, "Something else that's useful is a tent."

"A tent?"

"Yes, son. How would you like to help me put up a tent?"
He smiled. "Once we have it up, Grandma might make us
some lemonade for a little camp-treat."

"Oh boy, Grandpa!" I said.

I found out that Grandpa was good at putting up tents.
He let me hammer some of the pegs into the ground
to hold the sides down.

I helped him lay out the poles, and we decided which ones
were for the sides and which ones held up the awning.

As soon as the tent was up, Grandpa rolled up the window flaps
and tied them so that the wind could get in.

We finished with the tent just as Grandma brought out
her homemade lemonade.

I drank mine slowly, but Grandpa was done in a minute.
"Now, how about a gizmo for our tent?" he asked. "You stay here;
I've got just the thing."

He went into the house and came back carrying an old shoe box.

"This is a special little gizmo," he said in a hushed voice.
"I've had this one for a long time."

He opened the box and folded back the paper.
Then he took out a dangling thing of strings and glass.
He held it up and straightened out the parts that hung down.
He blew on it, and I heard a clear, tinkling tune.

"Let me try, Grandpa!" I said.

"Just blow gently. It doesn't take much wind," he said.

So I blew, and there was the tinkling again.

"This is a wind chime," Grandpa said.
"It's one of my favorite gizmos. Let's hang it up here."
He tied it inside the tent, right at the highest part of the roof.

Then we lay back on the floor and listened as the chime gizmo
made its music with the wind that blew through the tent windows.

"Grandpa," I asked, "could we camp out in the tent tonight,
just you and me?"
"Mmm," Grandpa said thoughtfully. "It should be a good night
for camping. But we've got some work to do first. We'll have to move
our bedding into the tent and get our flashlights ready.
Will you help me?"

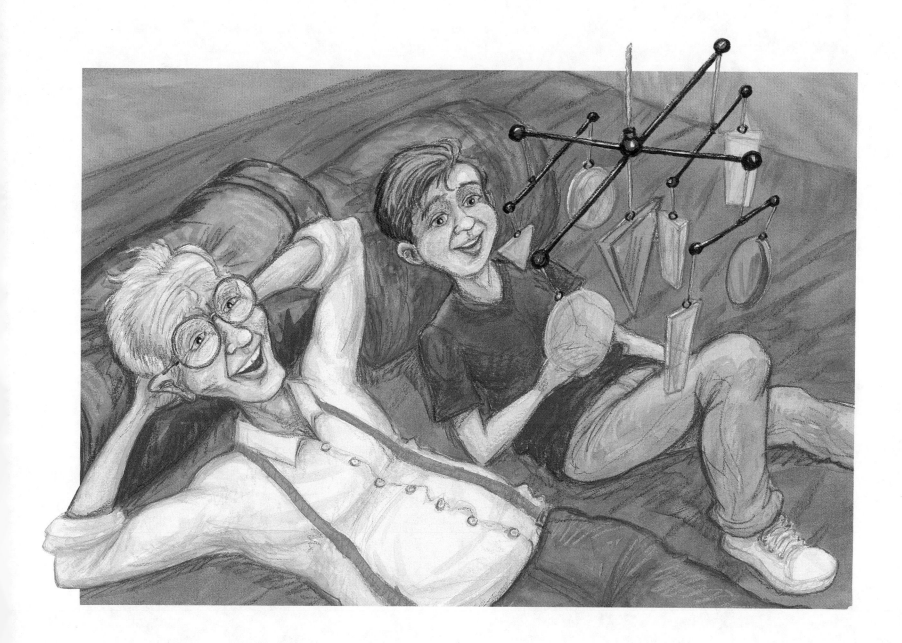

"Yes sir, Grandpa!" I said.

We carried pillows and blankets to the tent. I helped Grandpa
find two flashlights and check the batteries to make sure they worked.
Then we unpacked air mattresses and found an air pump
in a box in the garage. We stayed busy until supper time.

After supper, Grandma said I had to take a bath
before I could go out to the tent with Grandpa.
But I hurried; so it didn't take very long.

The sky was turning orange and red as we
settled down in the tent at last.

Grandpa and I lay on our stomachs
and watched the sunset colors change.

The gizmos in the yard started to change their colors too.
The windsock on the gazebo was still blowing steadily,
but now it looked dark against the red sky.

The pinwheels were still turning, and the flags were still waving,
but they seemed gray in the fading light.

The ribbons in the streamer tree kept on streaming
even though I couldn't tell them apart anymore.
Little by little, everything outside grew dark.

Inside the tent, Grandpa and I listened to the chime
as it tinkled its gizmo music. I didn't mind the dark
because Grandpa was there and we could talk.
And we had our gizmo music all to ourselves.

Or did we?

"Grandpa," I asked. "Can other people hear our chime gizmo?"

"Oh, I suppose they can, if they listen for it," he said.

"But Grandpa, I thought the gizmo music was for you and me."

"Of course it is, son," he said.

"Then why don't we close the tent flaps?
I want it just for us."

"You don't want any of it to get out?" he asked.

"No, Grandpa. I want to keep it just for you and me."

So Grandpa took his flashlight and went outside the tent.
He untied the straps and let the window flaps fall shut, one by one.

I could tell where he was because his flashlight
made a bright spot on the canvas as he worked his way
around the sides of the tent.

When he came back in, he zipped up the door flaps too.
Now we were really alone, just Grandpa and me
and our wind chime gizmo.

I settled back down on my blanket. It seemed very quiet.

We could talk, if we wanted to, and shine our lights,
but we couldn't see Grandpa's gizmos anymore.

I asked him if he thought the bleach bottles
were still turning on their sticks in the flower bed
and if the pinwheels on the rail of the gazebo were still spinning.

I asked him if the ribbons in the streamer tree
were still blowing like waves on the water
and if the paddles were still moving my gizmo's widget.

"As long as the wind is blowing, those gizmos are working,"
Grandpa said.

But with the tent flaps closed,
not even Grandpa could see the gizmos;
so we couldn't tell for sure.

Since we couldn't see any of the gizmos outside,
I decided to shine my flashlight on our chime gizmo inside.
That's when I noticed that it had stopped working.

For a while I just lay there in the quiet,
keeping my light on the chime gizmo. It hung silent and still.
What about the gizmos outside? Had they stopped too?

I wondered about that,
and I felt kind of lonely without the gizmo music.
"Grandpa?"

"Yes, son?"

"Let's look outside and see if the gizmos are still going."

Grandpa unzipped the door flaps, and we both looked out.
The night was too dark to see much, but right away
the wind got into our tent.
It stirred a faint, tinkling sound from the wind chime.

"Your chime gizmo, Grandpa! It's working!"

I listened to it for a while.
Sometimes the tinkling stopped.
Then it began again.
Then it stopped.

I had an idea.

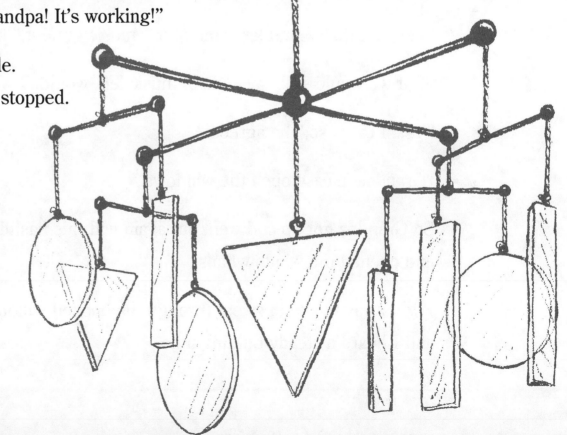

"Grandpa?"

"Mm-humm?"

"When we opened the door flap, our chime gizmo started working for a while. Do you think it would help to open the window flaps too?"

"Yes, but that would let some of our music get out," he said.

"But we would still have lots of music left, wouldn't we, Grandpa?"

"Yes, I think so," he agreed.

"Grandpa, please open the windows."

So Grandpa got up and went out again with his flashlight and opened the window flaps.

Right away the wind swept through the opened windows, and I heard a steady tinkling tune.

Grandpa came back into the tent as I was shining my light
on the wind chime, watching it work.

"You like to shine your light on that little gizmo, don't you?" he asked.

"I sure do, Grandpa."

"Take a look outside," he said quietly.

Up in the sky, just above the streamer tree, the moon had come out.
It was shining its silvery light on the gizmos in the yard.

I could see the windsock again, on top of the gazebo,
and the spinning pinwheels on the rail.
The moon shone on the flags waving up on the pole
and on my gizmo's widget, pumping up and down.

I turned off my flashlight and lay beside Grandpa
to watch the gizmos working in the moonlight.

"Grandpa?" I said with a yawn.

"Yes, son?"

"It's a good thing we opened the windows, huh?"

"Yes, son, I think you're right," he said.

And I could hear that I was right,
by the clear tinkling of our little wind chime.